D0984012

illustrated by
Barry Goldberg

written by
Mimi Mazzarella

For my sweeties ~ Aidan and Taylor
For my mom ~ Mildred Amodeo Fetta
And definitely ~ Barry Goldberg and Debby Peoples

M. M.

For my Mom and Dad

B.G.

STORYBOOK
GENIUS PUBLISHING
sbgpublishing.com

yip jar Book
Design by
yipjar.com

The annual Flower Festival was the crème de la crème of all garden affairs. Every rose, daisy, lilac and hundreds of other flora were eager to attend the up-and-coming event!

This year, it was particularly exciting for Iris who was going to the festival for the very first time. She was finally old enough and could not contain her youthful excitement!

Saturday

Flower Festival

FLOWERS ONLY!!

"I'm going to the festival!" she sang out to each flower she happened to see.
"That's just rosy!" called back Calla Lily. "I'll look for you there!"

"You're so grown up and have really blossomed," sighed Mari Gold.
"I remember when you were just a bulb!"
"Make sure you boogie a lot," laughed Daffy Dil.
"You don't wanna be a wallflower."

"Would you tell me more about the festival?" Iris begged Girly-Girl, a gorgeous purple and white "sister iris" who gave off a scent that was incredibly sweet-smelling.

Girly-Girl grinned. "Again?
Okay, you little pistil," she laughed.

"First, you should know that this is
the finest Flower Festival there is!"

"What goes on at this celebration?"
asked Iris.

"They give out awards, trophies and prizes,"
said Girly-Girl.

"In fact, this year I happen to know that I'm getting a blue ribbon for having the prettiest patterns on my petals. And Girly-Girl is getting a gold cup for her exquisite fragrance," chimed in Peggy Ann, a stunning purple iris with beautiful white streaks.

"How perfectly enchanting," sighed Iris.
"Maybe I'll win something, too."

"Who knows? Maybe you will,"
smiled Peggy Ann.

"Iris, the festival will be here before you know it," said Rosalie. "Have you found a friend to go with you?"

"I do know who I want to invite...but I haven't asked him yet," replied Iris.

"Who is he?" asked Rosalie.

"All I'm going to say is that his name is Dan."

Dan DeLion was an orphan. Somehow his wild seedling had blown into the garden. Now, at eighteen inches tall, he stood out as a big yellow weed among the divine purple irises. Because of this, he was often bullied by others.

Just recently, an iris named Hollywood Nights called Dan "Weedy," and then added, "You're not good enough to be on this playground. Now **GET OFF MY SEAT!**"

Dan tried hard not to let such prickly words bother him, so he looked at Iris.
"It's okay, Dan. Don't let him upset you," said Iris.

Dan felt better just knowing that his friend Iris was with him.
She gave him the strength to withstand those few foul flowers!
Thank heavens for Iris!

Later on the playground, Iris told Dan about the Flower Festival.

"Sounds like fun," he said.

"W-w-would you like to go with me?" gulped Iris,
as she blushed a deeper purple than she already was.

"Me?" Dan replied. "That's kind of an upmarket affair, isn't it?
I heard that weeds aren't permitted."

"The festival celebrates the beauty and joy that plants bring to the earth," answered Iris. "You have a sunny face and are always so happy, so why shouldn't you be allowed to go? Besides I don't want to bring anyone else."

"Okay, I'll go..." sighed Dan, "but just for you."

The big day had arrived and the two friends were on their way to the Flower Festival...
but Dan was getting cold leaves.

"What if they won't let me in?" he worried. "I'm not a flower."
"Don't be silly," smiled Iris. "You look like the sunshine!"
"That doesn't matter. There are too many of me," Dan sighed.

Iris felt bad about Dan's view of himself. She also knew that the other plants at the festival might make fun of him. But she hoped that evolution by now had taught them that all plants—even weeds—serve a purpose...and that makes them beautiful.

"So what's the big deal if you grow everywhere?" she asked.
"Because," he fretted, "it makes me run-of-the-mill...a dime a dozen."

The way that Dan thought about himself made Iris feel awful.
"I'm sorry," she said.
"No need for you to feel bad," he sighed. "It's not your fault that you were born so awesome. I wish I were a **true** flower...any kind...tulip...orchid...marigold."

When they got to the entrance, there was a super-sized sunflower at the trellis gate.

"Can you tell me where I go?" asked Dan.

"**YOU STAND BY YOURSELF!**
We don't usually get your kind here!" snapped the bouncer.

"But...he's with me," said Iris.
"That was not the best idea, Iris. Weeds don't belong here."
"I'm sorry to disagree with you. He's my friend, and I invited him,"
Iris said as the two friends walked past the bouncer and into the festival.

As the two friends walked in farther, they saw the angry faces on the flowers.

"This was not a good idea," Dan whispered to Iris.

"I'm getting foul-fertilizer glares from everyone."

"Ignore them," instructed Iris. "You're better than them all."

UNDESIRABLE!

Iris grabbed Dan's leaf
in hers, and the two
briskly walked away.

But it was awful.
Everywhere they went they
were snubbed and scorned.

When the pair went near the Tulip Troop, the tulips all grabbed
their bulbs and rushed to the other side of the room.

As they passed the Peace Lily Pack,
each lily raised a leafy fist in protest.

And, when the Baby's Breath Bunch saw them
coming close they—of course—cried, "WAA!"
The two friends were left to stand by themselves in
a far off corner as the Flower Festival began.

The first speaker of the evening was a red zinnia named Cherry Queen.
She was the coordinator of the festival.

ANNUAL FLOWER FESTIVAL

"We've all been told," Cherry said in a rich, vibrant voice, "that plants produce flowers for the sole purpose of making seeds and perpetuating themselves."

"However, we all know that flowers do more! We help to glorify the earth. We're beautiful! We're exotic! We're grand!"

"And...we also supply the air with sweet smells better than any perfume that man can make. Just think of what the world would be like without us."

Then it was time for the awards!
The Most Attractive ~ The Most Aromatic ~ The Most Unique, and so on. Each winner, of course, gave a very fragrant thank you speech.

"And the **Best Looking in the Rock Garden** goes to...Ritzy Rose!" Ritzy accepted her award, but as she started to give her speech---she noticed Iris and Dan.

"Thank you, thank you," she declared. "I'm so proud to be among such fabulous flowers and win the **Best Looking** award. However, it seems we have a **thorny** situation here. This annual Flower Festival is for cultivated **FLOWERS ONLY**, but it appears that we have a woebegone **WEED** among us."

Some of the audience gasped. Others looked around for the offending plant.

Gladys Gladiolus stood up and yelled, "You're right, sister! The weed needs to be removed. Who is it? Where is it?"

Ritzy pointed her leaf directly at Dan. "It's that dandelion over **THERE!**"

All heads turned towards Dan and Iris.
The sunflower bouncer who had been at
the entrance began to lumber over towards them.

The other flowers began chanting,
"GET THEM OUT! GET THEM OUT!"

Dan suddenly felt the courage to yell,

"ALL OF YOU QUIET!"

Every flower, surprised by his THUNDEROUS voice, got quiet.

"MY NAME IS DAN DELION," he said. "I came here today because my friend Iris invited me. I knew that I'd probably not be welcomed, but..."

At this point, the sunflower bouncer grabbed one of Dan's leaves.

"WAIT!" called out Cherry Queen.
"Let's hear what he has to say."
The bouncer let go and stood back.

"Thank you, Ms. Queen," replied Dan as he adjusted his bloom. "I know you think I'm only a common weed and don't deserve a place among you. However, I—and so many of my brothers and sisters who are scattered all over the world—should not be rejected."

"Why not?" challenged Supertunia Petunia.
"You're wild and coarse."

"You're wrong," spoke up Iris. "Dan is sweet and
gentle. In the day, he resembles the sun. And at
night, he curls up into a crescent, like the moon."

"What about the ugly
puff ball he turns into
once he's gone to seed?"
interrupted Ritzy Rose.

"Those seeds, once blown into the air...look like stars," said Iris.
"And besides, did any of you ever watch children blow on dandelion puff balls?"

All the flowers were silent as Iris continued. "If you did, then you'd hear them giggling at the wisps of stars as they float up and sail softly into the sky."

"It's magical. And if you don't think that's a thing of beauty, then you're just a bunch of snobs," said Iris.

Dan looked at Iris and blushed as much as a dandelion could.

"And one last thing, if I may add," she smiled.
"Bees of all kinds visit dandelions for nectar and pollen! Plus, these
fabulous free-spirits improve soil quality. Not to mention, they're edible.
So now what do you think of this lowly weed?" asked Iris.

Then she whispered over to her friend,
"Sorry about the edible part, Dan."

"LET'S HEAR IT FOR THE DANDELIONS!"

Immediately, cheers and hoots erupted. The festival was ablaze with congratulations and praise for Dan, who was beside himself with joy.

When he grabbed for Iris's leaf in appreciation, she whispered to him, "Too bad they never knew this about you."

"Well, sometimes feeling too proud of ourselves stops us from understanding what others are feeling," he smiled quietly.

It's the way of
Nature

CPSIA information can be obtained
at www.ICGtesting.com
Printed in the USA
LVHW071945051118
596007LV00027B/542/P